Mrs. Bannister started talking about what was going to happen all year, and my head began to swim. She handed out assignment books, journal notebooks, and what seemed like fifteen different textbooks. She told us the schedule for the day and then she gave a lecture on how she wanted our papers to look.

"There are only two things that really upset me, class. I'm going to tell you right up front so there's no mystery about it. One is bugs, and the other is papers without any name on them. Make sure I don't see any of either this year, and we'll get along just fine."

Unfortunately, I loved bugs and I never remembered to put my name on my paper. I wondered how Mrs. Bannister and I were going to get along. . . .

Ask for these titles from Chariot Books:
Project Cockroach
The Best Defense
Adam Straight to the Rescue
Adam Straight and the Mysterious Neighbor
Mystery on Mirror Mountain
Courage on Mirror Mountain

A JOSH McINTIRE BOOK

PROJECT COCKROACH

Elaine K. McEwan

Chariot Books™
David C. Cook Publishing Co.

To the fourth-, fifth-, and sixth-grade kids at Lincoln School

Chariot Books™ is an imprint of David C. Cook Publishing Co.
David C. Cook Publishing Co., Elgin, Illinois 60120
David C. Cook Publishing Co., Weston, Ontario
Nova Distribution, Ltd., Torquay, England

PROJECT COCKROACH

Cover design by Elizabeth Thompson
Cover illustration by Mel Williges
First printing, 1991
Printed in the United States of America
95 94 93 92   5 4 3 2

Library of Congress Cataloging-in-Publication Data
McEwan, Elaine K.
    Project Cockroach: a Josh McIntire Book/ by Elaine K.
McEwan
        p.   cm.
    Summary: After great resistance, Josh, a new student with
an interest in bugs, befriends nerdy Wendell, who comes to
Josh's aid during a crisis and introduces him to Christianity.
ISBN 1-55513-357-6
[1. Friendship—Fiction.2. Insects—Fiction. 3. Schools—Fiction
4. Christian life—Fiction.]   I. Title
PZ7.M4784545Pr 1991   91-11221
[Fic]—dc20   CIP
                                              AC

"Hey, you wanna go to the library with me?"

The voice came from the other side of the fence, but I couldn't see its owner through the overgrown shrubbery.

"It's me! Over here. Do you wanna go to the library with me or not?"

Who goes to the library in the summertime? Ugh! That's almost as bad as taking a shower every day.

I only take showers when my mother nags at me—and even then I sometimes just run water over my hair so it *looks* like I've showered.

"I can't!" I called back. "I have to help my mom unpack."

"Well, maybe you can make it tomorrow. See you later." The voice and its owner vanished.

What kind of weirdo was my next-door neighbor? Not only did this oddball go to the library in the summertime, he went two days in a row! We were definitely not living on the same planet.

"Joshua, get in here, please! I need some help right now."

My mom was all freaked out about cleaning the house. Even though we're just renting, she says she wants to make it as nice as possible. But no matter how much she cleans this dump, it's never going to look as good as our old place. I've already counted seventeen cockroaches behind the refrigerator, and I haven't tried to keep track of all those in the basement, let alone the spiders and earwigs. The place is an entomologist's paradise.

Entomologists study bugs. I learned all about them in science last year when we made a bug collection. I got an A on that assignment. It was the most fun I've ever had in school.

"Joshua, will you get in here immediately? I can't do everything on my own."

Mom sounded as though she might burst into tears any second. Ever since my dad moved out in February, she's done more crying than laughing.

I found her in the living room. "Joshua McIntire at your service. How may I help you, madam?"

A brief smile crossed her face. Maybe it wasn't going to be all bad with just the two of us. I could be the man of the family. I knew how to change fuses, catch cockroaches, and make my mom smile.

"Did I hear voices outside? Who was it?" Mom asked.

"I'm not sure—the bushes are so thick I couldn't actually see a person. I think it was the boy next door, but I'm not going to bother to meet him. You know what he wanted to do? Go to the library. Nobody goes to the library in the summertime."

"Joshua, I can't believe your attitude. Maybe if you went to the library more often, you'd get better grades in school. The real estate agent told me about the family next door. They've lived there for seven years. Wendell is a perfectly nice young man—"

At the sound of his name, I doubled over in laughter. "Wendell! Did you say Wendell? Nobody has a name like Wendell. What's his last name, Weird? Wendell Weird." I repeated the name several times. "That's perfect. I'll bet Weird Wendell washes his wig on windy winter Wednesdays."

My mother was getting that thoroughly irritated look she puts on when I'm being rude or disrespectful. "That's enough, Joshua. Give him a chance. You're new in town and you need friends. We need friends. You can't just ignore your next-door neighbor."

"Maybe you can't, but I can. I don't need a friend named Wendell who reads books in the summertime, thank you."

I said the "thank you" with just the slightest hint of sarcasm in my voice. It was something I did when I got mad. I also get this silly grin on my face just

7

when I'm supposed to be serious—and it usually gets me into big trouble. I've been in the principal's office more than once for what he called my "disrespectful attitude." I always thought I was telling the truth, but adults don't always want to hear the truth. At least my version of it.

My mother didn't say anything else, but she was annoyed, and I knew the subject would come up again. There was something about the set of her chin and her pursed lips. Once she got an idea about something "right" I should do, she never left me alone. I knew she'd find a hundred sneaky ways to slip Wendell into the conversation until I finally gave in and met him.

But not today. Not on top of all the other stuff I was dealing with. After all, how many times in your life do your parents split up, so you have to move away from your Little League team and the house where you were born? How many times do you have to leave your best friend since kindergarten who knows everything there is to know about you? How many times do you have to start a new school where nobody knows you're the best dodge-ball player in the western hemisphere? I sure hoped it wouldn't be more than once, because once was about all I could handle.

My dad always said that when you're feeling down, you should go for a walk or a bike ride. Dad is an auto parts salesman. Whenever he got discouraged about not selling any auto parts, which was a lot of the time, he'd say, "Physical exercise is a good antidote for depression," and he'd put on his gym shoes and we'd jog around the block together. I decided to try his advice now.

"Mom," I said, with that pleasant and polite tone of voice that grown-ups love, "do you need anything from the grocery store? I can ride my bike up to the Convenient Mart and get a Coke with the leftover money."

I'm pretty independent for a ten year old. My grandma always yells at my mom for the way she lets me ride all over on my bike, but Mom trusts me. I let her know where I'm going, and I call if I end up going to somebody's house. I'd been doing it in our old neighborhood since I was eight.

She hesitated, then she gave in. "Well, I could use a quart of milk and some cream of mushroom soup."

"We're not having that gruesome tuna and noodle casserole again, are we?" I moaned.

"Joshua, we're on a tight budget. Until I get my first paycheck, we're going to be counting our pennies. But I guess you can have a Coke."

I can always tell when my mom is getting a "guilty attack." She was thinking she should say no because, after all, I was just rude and obnoxious, but

9

she was also feeling sorry for me and sort of guilty for getting divorced and taking me away from my friends. I try to save this kind of pressure for stuff that's really important, but getting out of the house right now seemed to qualify.

The Convenient Mart was just down the street. The counter man looked a little mysterious and dangerous. He gave me the creeps as his dark eyes followed me up and down the aisles until I found the milk and cream of mushroom soup. I couldn't figure out if he thought I was going to take something or if he just didn't have anything better to do.

If Mom ever found out about some of the magazines they have behind the counter here, I'm not sure she'd let me come back. But for now, the Coke was cold and the air conditioning felt great. I looked longingly at the video games, but I didn't have any money left over. Beside, my mom would kill me if she knew I was playing video games. She says they aren't a "productive use of time."

It was tempting to keep on riding toward town, but I knew the milk would spoil, so I headed for home. I was balancing the bag and trying to park my bike on the front porch when I heard a voice. I looked up to see a tall, skinny kid walking up the front steps.

"Hi. I'm your next-door neighbor, Wendell Hathaway."

What rotten luck. I thought of clever responses I could make, but I didn't need my mouth washed out with soap today. And I knew my mother would ground me if I wasn't polite to Wendell, so I answered.

"Hi."

Wendell didn't look anything like I'd pictured him. He was worse. If only we could have continued our acquaintance with the fence between us.

He was wearing brown leather shoes with rubber soles, polyester pants, and an awful green plaid shirt. What fashion sense. His wardrobe alone made him certifiably weird, even without the plastic grocery bag full of books he was carrying. And if that wasn't enough, his hair looked like it was styled by Schmitz Lawn and Garden Service.

Wendell thrust his hand out. "How do you do?"

Oh no, I thought. He actually shakes hands. I couldn't stand it. Now my mother would have the perfect example of politeness to throw in my face every time I said the wrong thing. His eager-beaver attitude made me want to throw up.

I didn't know whether to shake his hand or run into the house, but once again my good judgment prevailed. I shook hands with Wendell, hoping that this simple act would fulfill all of my social obligations for the next hundred years.

11

"I have to get this milk inside right away. It's going to spoil." I raced into the house at top speed, slammed the door, and breathed a sigh of relief.

"You're not going to believe Wendell Hathaway, Mom. He is truly unreal. His clothes look like Salvation Army rejects, and he wears rubber-soled shoes! My old social studies teacher wore rubber-soled shoes. He had bad feet. And brown. Do you believe it? Nobody wears brown shoes."

My mother waited until I had finished my speech, then she quietly said, "Maybe Wendell has bad feet, too. And remember, Joshua, you can't always tell a book by its cover." My mother has a famous saying for every occasion.

She followed up that gem with another zinger. "Handsome is as handsome does."

Well, Wendell was going to have to *do* a lot as far as I was concerned to move into the handsome category. At this point, he hadn't even made acceptable.

I had been looking forward to school. I wanted to make some friends so I'd have someone to hang out with. Now, with Wendell in the picture, I was as thrilled about the first day of school as I'd be about a visit to the dentist. I groaned just thinking of it.

It's hard to know what to wear on the first day at a new school. I wanted to look good, but not too good. My Chicago Cubs shirt was clean, and the team was in first place in the National League, so that made up my mind. I also had a new pair of jeans that didn't even look new.

My mom was full of all sorts of good advice. "Now, I want you to be nice to Wendell."

"Aw, Mom. Let me check out the scene at school first. I'm embarrassed to live next door to him, let alone be seen talking to him."

"Joshua, we're not going to have this discussion every morning. I'm late for work."

Going back to work was not something Mom had planned to do for a long while yet. She was an executive secretary, whatever that means, at the Associated Foods Company. They make cereals and stuff like that. Some nights the neighborhood smells like a bakery, when the wind is blowing in the right direction. It always makes me hungry, even if I've just finished dinner.

"We'll talk about this later. Just promise you won't get into trouble on the first day, okay?" She sounded a little desperate.

"I promise, Mom."

"Here's your lunch money." She gave me a quick kiss and was out the door.

Now I had to figure out how to get to school without running into Wendell. Maybe if I sneaked out the back door and through the alley, he wouldn't see me.

I don't know what I expected to find when I got to Jefferson School, but I sure was surprised. It looked like a political convention on the playground. There were all kinds of people waving signs, and everybody was laughing and talking. All except for me. The thought crossed my mind, but only for a second, that maybe I should have waited for Wendell. At least he was one person I knew.

I was ready to turn around and go back home when somebody with a clipboard tapped me on the shoulder. She was friendly looking, with a wide smile.

"Hi, I don't recognize you. I'm Mrs. Wescott, the music teacher. What's your name?"

"Joshua McIntire."

"What grade are you in, Joshua?"

"Fifth."

"Well, just let me take at look at my official list and find out whose class you're in. Have you already registered?"

I nodded. Mom had been in a couple of weeks earlier to sign me up.

"Ah, yes, you're right here on Mrs. Bannister's list. Do you know anybody here at Jefferson?"

I didn't want to admit I knew Wendell Hathaway, so I just shrugged and hoped she wouldn't wait for an answer.

"Well, Joshua, we're really glad to have you here. Jefferson is a great school. Why don't you see if you can find Mrs. Bannister? She'll be carrying a big sign with her name on it."

I thanked Mrs. Wescott and went off to find my new teacher.

Mrs. Bannister was easy to spot. She was a good foot taller than any of the other adults on the playground and was wearing a huge sun hat. Springy gray curls stuck out around the edges of the hat, and she was wearing Reeboks. She had a whistle, a pair of glasses, and one of those mechanical pencils all hanging around her neck on assorted chains and holders. She wasn't going to waste any time looking for what she needed!

She took one look at me and said, "You're new to Jefferson, aren't you? Are you in my class?"

I nodded.

She consulted her clipboard and immediately came up with my name. "I'll bet you're Joshua McIntire."

I was amazed and could only nod again. She probably thought I couldn't talk.

"Well, what do you think of our school, Joshua?"

I was too busy wondering how she knew who I was to even think of anything to say. While I was stammering, she answered her own question.

"I'm sure you'll like it."

Well, one thing was certain. Everybody seemed to think this school was something special. That was a good sign.

"Joshua, let me introduce you to someone from our class," Mrs. Bannister continued. "We're waiting for everybody to get here before we go inside."

I knew it. The first person Mrs. Bannister laid eyes on was Wendell Hathaway.

"Wendell's one of our top students, Joshua. I know you'll enjoy getting to know him."

Wendell eyed me with a strange expression. "Joshua and I have already met, Mrs. Bannister."

Mrs. Bannister didn't seem to notice how uncomfortable we both were. She moved on to greet some parents and left me alone with Wendell. My mother's parting words echoed in my ears: "Be polite to Wendell." Since there wasn't anyone else around, I guessed it couldn't hurt.

"Do you know what Mrs. Bannister's nickname is?" Wendell asked. "Buggy Bannister."

"Is she crazy or something?"

"Oh, no," said Wendell. "She's a pretty good teacher. But she goes on a rampage whenever she finds bugs in her room. She makes everybody empty their desks, and she goes on a search and destroy mission. Everybody who's ever been in her room thinks it's a real blast. Class just shuts down until every bug is gone. I'm real interested in bugs."

Wendell was interested in bugs, too? I wondered if he wanted to be an entomologist. I forgot my pledge not to talk to him.

"My mom has sure found a lot of varieties in our house," I said.

More kids were crowding around Mrs. Bannister and her sign. She blew her whistle, and everyone stopped talking.

"All right, class. We're going inside the building for the first time of the school year. I expect you to enter quietly and in a straight line. I have name tags on each desk for today, but don't worry if your desk doesn't fit. We'll rearrange things as we need to. Okay . . . forward, march."

We all fell into line behind the tall teacher with

the strange hat and the Reeboks. The school year had begun.

I felt a little funny in my stomach. I wasn't sure if it was because I hadn't eaten enough for breakfast or if the whole idea of starting a new school was getting to me.

Wendell's seat was across the room. Thank goodness, I didn't have to deal with him close up right away. Even though we had two things in common—our address and bugs—I still couldn't stand the way he looked. Those rubber-soled shoes were too much. Even the teacher wore Reeboks. I wondered why Wendell didn't get with it. He seemed like a smart enough kid. Didn't he know that everybody wore tennis shoes?

I didn't have time to think about Wendell, because Mrs. Bannister began talking about what was going to happen all year, and my head began to swim. She handed out assignment books, journal notebooks, and what seemed like fifteen different textbooks. I would never be able to fit it all into this puny desk. She told us the schedule for the day and then she gave a lecture on how she wanted our papers to look.

"There are only two things that really upset me, class. I'm going to tell you right up front so there's no mystery about it. One is bugs and the other is papers without any name on them. Make sure I don't see any of either this year, and we'll get along just fine."

Wendell was right on about Mrs. Bannister. She seemed like an okay teacher, but she knew what she didn't like. Unfortunately, I loved bugs and I never remembered to put my name on my paper. I wondered how Mrs. Bannister and I were going to get along.

Our first assignment was journal writing. I'd never heard of journals before, so I was glad when somebody else asked a question about what we were supposed to do.

Mrs. Bannister explained. "Each day, class, we'll take five or ten minutes to write in our journals. I will suggest a possible topic, or you can write about anything you want to. No one will read your journal unless you give permission. Writing every day will give you practice and help you become better writers. The only rule is that everyone writes during journal time."

We didn't do anything like this in my other school. The funny feeling in my stomach was getting worse. I wondered if they had a nurse's office here. Maybe I was getting the flu and should have my temperature taken. I sure hoped I wouldn't throw up on the first day in a new school.

The journal topic Mrs. Bannister assigned was something I'd written about on the first day of every school year since second grade: "How I Spent My Summer Vacation." Why couldn't teachers be more original?

I guessed maybe I could think up five minutes' worth of summer activity, although I didn't have an actual vacation this year. And I could be truthful, since nobody was going to read it.

My summer vacation was rotten. My mom and dad got divorced, and I moved from my old house. I miss my friends, and Wendell Hathaway is the only person I've met. That's worse than not meeting anybody at all. I don't know when I'll see my dad again, and my stomach really hurts.

I couldn't believe the time was up already. Maybe journal writing wouldn't be as bad as I thought.

It was time for gym. Once again we hit the halls, but only after Mrs. Bannister warned us about the "no talking" rule. I'd never heard so many rules.

The gym teacher, Mrs. Borthistle, greeted us at the gym door wearing a whistle and Reeboks. Whistles and Reeboks were apparently the "in" things at Jefferson this year. Too bad Wendell hadn't gotten the message.

We divided into teams for dodge ball, and suddenly I felt good again. Dad was right. Physical activity is a good antidote for depression. At least there was one thing in this school I'd be able to do.

Now if I could just find a normal friend, I'd feel even better.

The minute Mom walked in the door, she wanted to know all about the first day of school.

"It was fine," I said. My theory is that you don't tell your mom more than you absolutely have to.

"Well, give me some details."

"What would you like to know?" I countered. She and I play this game often.

"Come on, Joshua. I want to know about your teacher, your class, the school, whatever. Just tell me something that lets me know you were actually in school today."

I told her about Mrs. Bannister and her distaste for anything with more than four legs.

Mom laughed. "She certainly wouldn't survive in this house for long. So, did you see Wendell?"

"Mom, do we have to discuss Wendell? I was polite, okay?"

She didn't press the point, and I didn't volunteer anything more.

"One more question. Is it going to be all right at Jefferson?"

I thought for a moment. "It's okay, I guess." I wasn't ready to commit myself one way or another.

Amazingly enough, I did feel like going back the next morning.

I put on my Chicago Bears shirt and ate some Fruit Loops. I love the way the milk turns a sickening pink color after the cereal soaks in it a few minutes. My Mom says it makes her feel nauseated.

I had time to shoot a few baskets before I left for school, but I'd forgotten one thing. Wendell. He appeared out of nowhere and looked at my backpack on the driveway expectantly.

"Are you ready to go?"

Wendell's outfit made him eligible for the Ten Worst Dressed Fifth Graders of the World. The shoes were the same, but today's pants were a gross green, and the shirt looked like soggy Fruit Loops. I felt nauseated myself. But there was no way I could avoid walking to school with him. Not if I intended to keep my promise to Mom.

We didn't say much to each other. I just kept hoping no one from my class would spot me. The walk took us through town, past several small shops and a couple of taverns. One of the shops had a white leather coat in the window. It looked like something a rock star would wear.

We passed the train station and headed into the dark and musty underpass that provided safe passage under the railroad tracks. The walls were covered with graffiti, and I thought I could make out Mrs. Bannister's name in the scribbled mess. The commuter train to the city rumbled overhead, and the sudden appearance of a bearded man walking toward us made me glad I wasn't alone. But the minute we hit the sidewalk in front of school, I mumbled, "See you in class, Wendell," and ran to the playground.

I was looking for Ben Anderson. He was the only kid who had dared to question Mrs. Bannister's explanation of the rules yesterday. I wished I'd had the nerve to say what he did.

The bell rang, and everyone ran to line up. Maybe I'd have a chance to talk to Ben at recess.

Other teachers I've had sort of eased into the school year, but not Mrs. Bannister. She was all business. She assigned three pages of math, a report on explorers in the New World, and a paragraph on our idea of a perfect day. And that was all before lunch.

I decided to use the study period to begin my paragraph. My pencil needed sharpening, and on the way back to my seat I walked by Ben's desk. He had the lid up and was fiddling with what looked like a jug of water. Maybe I could ask him about it at recess.

Mrs. Bannister was meeting with a small group of students at the front of the room and glanced my way with a questioning look in her eye. I hurried to my seat and got to work.

My idea of a perfect day is one with no school.

Maybe I was getting carried away with the truth. I'd been in trouble at my old school for being too honest. I crumpled up the paper and put my name on a new sheet.

My idea of a perfect day will be when my mother and father get back together again.

This try wasn't much better than the first one. I didn't want anyone to know how bad I felt about my parents' divorce. I crumpled the second sheet. Out of the corner of my eye I could see Mrs. Bannister walking up the aisle. I took out a third sheet of paper.

"What's the matter, Joshua? Are you having a hard time getting started on your assignment?"

I couldn't tell Mrs. Bannister that I kept having second thoughts about what I was writing. I just smiled and said, "Nah, I'm fine." I'd just had a great idea.

My idea of a perfect day is when the Cubs win the World Series, the Chicago Bears win the Super Bowl, and my Little League team just plain wins a game.

I was on a roll now. Sports was my topic. The classroom was quiet, and the warm breezes and the

September sunshine were kind of relaxing. Suddenly there was a commotion near the front of the room. Two girls were screaming.

One of them was Tracy Kendall. She didn't look like the screaming type to me, but there she was with her red ponytail bobbing, shouting, "Gross! Oh, isn't that just the grossest thing you've ever seen?"

Tracy's opinion was seconded by someone else whose name I couldn't remember. "Ben Anderson, if you don't get that out of here right away, I'm going to throw up on your desk."

The class immediately went out of control. Kids started running toward Ben's desk, and more screams and shouts filled the air. Mrs. Bannister had a plan for just such emergencies. The whistle that hung around her neck for playground supervision shrilly sounded. The room fell dead quiet.

"Now, Ben, suppose you show me just what is causing all of this commotion."

Ben proudly produced his "show and tell." His plastic Pepsi bottle contained a dead frog floating in the murky water. It was all puffed out and looked like one of those giant balloons in the Macy's Thanksgiving Day parade.

I agreed with Tracy. It was gross. My normally strong stomach did a little flip-flop, and I was glad it was before lunch and not after. But I really had to hand it to Ben. He knew how to liven up a morning.

Mrs. Bannister was not amused. Ben and his frog were banished to the principal's office. Even though Mrs. Bannister went with him, no one said another word. Her shrill whistle and harsh look had sent a strong message. She was clearly in control.

But secretly each of us was wondering, "How did Ben get that frog in the bottle?"

After lunch Mrs. Bannister began reading aloud. She seemed to have forgotten the frog incident. Her voice was soothing, and she used a lot of expression. I'd never done that much reading outside of school assignments, but the book she was reading sounded really interesting. Maybe I'd see if the public library had a copy. I'd noticed that Wendell always had his nose in a book. When did he do his homework?

We started science, but I found it hard to concentrate on the differences between the digestive, respiratory, and circulatory systems. I was thinking how tonight I'd really have something interesting to tell Mom at dinner. Little did I know that the best was yet to come.

I was the first person to notice that we had a visitor in the classroom. The hairy creature made his way in stops and starts down the aisle. I didn't say a word . . . I wasn't looking for trouble.

The intruder got closer to my desk. I recognized

it as *Blatella germanica*. The bug book I'd gotten for my birthday from my grandpa and grandma was full of that kind of information. Charlie Simpson, in the seat next to mine, recognized it by its more common name and didn't have the same self-control I did. He waved his arm in the air.

Mrs. Bannister was talking and did not like to be interrupted. He waved more wildly and then took the plunge. "Mrs. Bannister, there's a cockroach crawling down the aisle."

Her expression that morning when she saw Ben's frog was positively delightful compared to how she looked now. It was not a pretty sight.

"Class, " she boomed, "we have a major problem here. I'm tired of these interruptions."

Personally, I didn't see what the problem was. We were doing science. Here was a perfect opportunity to study wildlife in its natural habitat.

"This is simply intolerable. I will not have bugs in my classroom." With each sentence her voice reached a higher pitch. I wondered if she might not have in mind exterminating a student or two along with the cockroach.

There were kids in the class whose older brothers and sisters had been in Mrs. Bannister's class, and they knew the routine. Everybody dumped out their desks, book bags, and lunch boxes, and turned their jackets inside out. The cupboard beneath the sink was emptied and a flashlight turned on its dark recesses. Tracy and Jamie were dispatched to the custodian's office to get some strong soap and water. We were on a search and destroy mission for bugs.

Mrs. Bannister was like a general looking for the enemy. Obviously her power reached to high places. The principal, Mrs. Raymond, was summoned, and she promised that the exterminator would be called at once.

When the three o'clock bell rang, I was exhausted. This was more work than studying.

Ben and I walked out of class together. This was the first time we had actually talked to each other, and I was eager to make a good impression.

"Do you believe how freaked out Mrs. Bannister gets about bugs and stuff?" I said.

Ben answered with a somewhat sinister smile. "I wonder what she'd do if she really saw a bunch of them? Remember that old movie, *Raiders of the Lost Ark*, with all those spiders? She'd probably get hysterical."

"Yeah, you're right," I said. "She sure wouldn't be able to live in my house. We've got tons of them—cockroaches, too."

"No kidding," Ben replied thoughtfully. "Wouldn't it be a riot to collect a whole bunch?"

I fixed myself my favorite snack—peanut butter and jelly on toast. I had plenty of homework to do, and I needed the energy. Mrs. Bannister had really been mad about all of the day's interruptions. She assigned three more things as homework to "make up for all the time we wasted today." If I wanted to keep my promise to Dad about getting good grades this quarter, I needed to buckle down early.

That thought reminded me that Dad hadn't called me yet, and I wondered when I'd get to see him again. He was two hundred miles away, and so far we hadn't worked out a schedule. This depressing thought, along with all of the homework I had to do, must have made me look pretty downhearted.

"Hey, big boy. What's the matter?" My mom breezed in with a cheery ring to her voice. Just seeing her crinkly smile made me feel better.

"Aw, Mom, I'm just tired. You're not gonna believe what happened in school today." I wasn't going to play the question and answer game today. Before long we were both laughing so hard the tears were rolling down our cheeks.

"I can't wait to meet this lady," she said. "She is certainly different from any teacher you've had before. I think I'm going to like her."

I felt better and decided to postpone my homework until later. Mom said I could ride my bike to town if I promised to be home by five. I wanted to check out that weird leather coat and the Mexican grocery store on Main Street.

Grandville was definitely a more interesting place to live than my old town. There was the karate school with its mysterious smells and sounds, the train yard with miles of box cars and switches, and the hardware store with the bait machine out front. All of them held the promise of adventure. What a shame it was September and not June. School was definitely going to interfere with having a good time.

Not only did the leather coat look like something a rock star would wear, but the man behind the counter inside actually looked like a rock star. He wore a fringed leather vest, and an earring dangled from his left ear. I stood in the doorway and stared.

"May I help you?" he inquired.

I was at a loss for words. How could I tell him I

just wanted to get a closer look at the white leather coat? I glanced at the window, and he seemed to read my mind.

"Interesting, isn't it? It was a custom order that somebody decided they didn't want. I don't know what I'm going to do with it."

Suddenly I could see my mom wearing that coat. "How much is it?" I asked.

"Fifteen hundred dollars. I'll probably never get my money out of it."

Fifteen hundred dollars sounded like a fortune to me. If I had that much money, my mom would probably want a new couch or car before she wanted a white leather coat. But it was fun to dream.

The proprietor walked over and stuck out his hand. "I'm Sonny Studebaker, and this is Studebaker's Leather Emporium. Have I seen you around town before?"

I wasn't sure how much information to give to Mr. Studebaker. Could he be the Stranger Danger type they always warned us about in school? But it would be fun to know someone with enough nerve to wear an earring.

"We just moved to town. I go to Jefferson School." I hadn't really told him much.

"What's your name?" he asked.

I began to get anxious. Mom would definitely not approve of this conversation. Visions of being kidnapped and never seeing my mother again raced through my mind. I looked at the clock on the wall and panicked.

"Hey, I'm late for supper. My mom is going to kill me."

I jumped on my bike, and as I pulled away, Mr. Studebaker yelled, "I'll put the coat on hold for you."

I took the long way home because I wanted to see if any karate classes were going on, and I squeaked in the door seconds before five o'clock. Mom was chopping up onions, and I could tell from the sizzling sound we were having hamburgers for supper.

"So how was town?" she asked. I wasn't sure how much to tell her.

"Fine," I answered. We were back to the question and answer game.

My excursion had used up the peanut butter and jelly energy, and I was really starved. Mom had all my favorite hamburger toppings—chili sauce, mustard, bean sprouts, olives, and hot peppers. Dad always had hot peppers on his hamburgers. There it was again—just when I least expected it, I thought of him again. Maybe he would call tonight.

The phone did ring while we were clearing the table, and I raced to pick it up.

"This is Wendell Hathaway. May I please speak to Joshua?"

He was polite even on the telephone. Maybe I

could pretend he had the wrong number. Or I could just hang up. But he had caught me off guard.

"Hi, Wendell." Too bad we hadn't kept our phone number unlisted. Now I'd never be safe.

"I was wondering if you wanted to go to church with me tonight. There's this group called Awana. We play games—"

I interrupted Wendell's prepared speech. Thank goodness I had a good excuse. I didn't even have to fib.

"I haven't done any of my homework yet. Sorry."

Wendell didn't seem at all disappointed. In fact, he was downright cheerful when he replied, "Oh, that's okay. Maybe you can go some other time."

I'd have to come up with a different excuse next week.

I spread my books out on the living room floor, scrunched up a sofa pillow under my elbows, and hit the remote control. This was where I did my best work. I'd seen "The Brady Bunch" reruns so many times I didn't need to watch. They kept me company while I worked. I'd just gotten everything arranged when the phone rang again. This would be Dad for sure.

Mom beat me to the phone. Maybe she was waiting for Dad to call, too.

"Joshua, it's for you again. You certainly are popular tonight."

It was Ben Anderson. Maybe having our phone number listed wasn't such a bad idea after all.

Ben didn't waste any time. "You know that idea about getting a whole bunch of bugs to scare Mrs. Bannister?"

"Uh huh. What about it?" I answered.

"Well, what if we did it?"

I was at once elated and terrified—elated that Ben had chosen me as an accomplice in this delicious plot, and terrified that I would get into trouble when I had promised my parents this would be a good year. The conflict between good and evil was settled very quickly.

"How would we do it?" I asked.

Ben had done his homework. And I don't mean reading and math. "You collect all the bugs at your house. Didn't you say you had a bunch?"

"Yes," I murmured, not wanting Mom to catch the drift of this conversation.

"Then we'll sneak into our class and put them in Buggy Bannister's desk," continued Ben. "It'll be spectacular."

I wasn't quite sure that was the right word, but I had to admit Ben's plan was appealing.

"So, what do you think? Do you wanna do it?" His voice was eager.

I could tell my mom was listening from across the room. I wanted to get off the phone fast.

"Sure," I mumbled. "That'll be fine."

"Okay," said Ben. "I'll see you at school tomorrow. We can figure everything out then."

I hung up the phone and waited for the inevitable question. Mom always seems to know when I'm uneasy about something.

"Who was that?" she wondered aloud.

"Just a kid in my class," I replied.

"What did he want?" Now she was into her interrogation mode.

"Nothing really." I was getting into dangerous territory. I needed to change the subject and get out.

"I hope you're using good judgment when it comes to friends, Joshua," my mother lectured. "If you get mixed up with the wrong kids, it could spoil your whole year."

"I'll be fine, Mom," I reassured her. "I'm in the fifth grade. I need to do my homework. You don't want me to get a detention, do you?"

My strategy worked, and she went back to balancing her checkbook.

I pretended to be busy with my homework, but I was actually thinking about Ben's plan. I had to admit it was better than anything I'd ever thought of. We had plenty of cockroaches down in the basement. I'd just have to figure out a way to convince Mom that we should cancel the exterminator she had coming on Friday.

At breakfast I brought up my idea.

"We have to do a science project, and I've been thinking about doing mine on cockroaches," I began.

I could tell by the look on her face that Mom didn't think much of the idea.

"I can't believe you're serious, Joshua. They are filthy and dangerous bugs."

This was going to take some selling. "But Mom, scientists need to know about these things. Maybe I can contribute to a cure for cockroaches." My voice took on a desperate tone. "Please, Mom," I begged. "Nobody else will have anything like it. I'll get an A in science."

That was the clincher. Mom loved good grades. Now, all I needed were some books and glass jars. . . .

Ben found me on the school playground. I had my first real friend at Jefferson.

"I talked my mom into letting me keep a bunch of the bugs for my science project," I told him.

He looked impressed. "When do you think we should do this?" he asked. "Tomorrow?"

Ben obviously didn't have the forethought I had.

"Oh, no," I said. "You have to give me some time to make this realistic. I'll need to check out some books and look like I'm writing a report. I don't want my mom to get suspicious. We'll do it next week."

I was committed. More than committed—I was out in front leading. I'd had some doubts before breakfast, but Ben's open admiration erased the last of them.

When Mrs. Bannister gave us time in the library learning center to do research for our reports, I found three books on cockroaches. The *1985 World Book* encyclopedia looked good, too. It had a three-page article and a great outline. I had no idea that cockroaches were so popular. I could hardly wait for the bell, so I could officially begin working on Project Cockroach.

Ben and I talked after school. "Why don't I come over and help you catch them?" he volunteered.

I didn't want to tell him that my mom had a rule about having friends in the house when she wasn't home, so I said I was busy.

He looked disappointed. "I'll call you later then," he said.

My first job was finding some containers. What I needed were some of those glass jars Mom used to can fruit in before she went back to work. I hoped she hadn't thrown them away. I could poke holes in the metal lids to give the cockroaches air and observe their behavior through the glass. For a minute I had forgotten the real purpose of my cockroach catching caper.

I found the jars in the pantry. I was beginning to get used to this house. It wasn't as fancy as the one we used to live in, but it had a lot of different little cupboards and closets for storing things. Our other house didn't have a basement, either. That's probably why we didn't have bugs.

I pulled the chain that turned on the bare light bulb over the basement stairs. They seemed much steeper than I remembered. The dank, musty odor reminded me of a cave we'd visited on a summer vacation once. Suddenly I wished I'd let Ben come over. The basement floor was an uneven dirt surface, and cobwebs hung from the wooden rafters.

I'll bet this place is at least a hundred years old, I thought. A shaft of sunlight came in through a broken window. I could see stacks of old *National Geographics* and a big metal trunk with rusty hinges in the far corner. I shivered a little and then decided I'd better get this over with.

There was a yardstick leaning up against the wall,

and I began to poke around behind the trunk. I wasn't disappointed. There were dozens of the fascinating creatures crawling on the wall. Boy, were they ugly. I suddenly realized that the only thing I had to pick them up with was my bare hands. I'm not usually squeamish, but now was not the time to prove my bravery. I looked briefly in the kitchen drawer, but decided that my mom's flour scoop would not be the best choice. I tried the garage. Someone had left an old garden trowel hanging on a pegboard. Perfect.

I decided to put on an old pair of gloves just in case one of the creatures got rambunctious. Also, I didn't know whether I was allergic to cockroaches or not, but one of the books I'd been reading said that lots of people are. I didn't want to wake up tomorrow morning with a strange rash.

The basement didn't seem quite as scary as it had earlier, and I got right to work. I had a bunch of jars, but I couldn't decide how many cockroaches I needed. For maximum shock effect, I guessed we'd want quite a few—maybe fifty or more—but I'd have a hard time explaining that many to Mom. I compromised and collected twenty, five in each of four jars. Maybe I'd do an experiment and feed them different foods or, even better, different roach killers. Yeah, I'd see which roach killer worked the fastest on them. On second thought, I really didn't like that idea. The cockroaches had a bizarre kind of appeal, and I just couldn't see killing them in cold blood.

I heard the phone ringing and raced up the stairs. I was still waiting for a call from Dad.

"Did you get 'em?" Ben asked excitedly.

"We're ready to go," I answered.

"How many?"

"Enough," I replied.

"When can I see them?" he wanted to know.

"Maybe later tonight. Why don't you come over after supper?" Knowing how Mom feels about checking with her first, I shouldn't have said that, but I didn't want to let a chance to get together with Ben slip away.

"Where do you live?" Ben wanted to know.

"Over on Kinney Ave."

"Doesn't that strange kid, Wendell, live over there?" he asked.

Oh, no, I thought. Here it goes. Once Ben finds out I live next door to Wendell, it will be all over. "Yeah, I guess so," I managed to choke out. "But I never see him."

"Okay, see you later," Ben promised.

I ran back down to the basement to put the last of my newfound friends in their temporary residence.

The phone rang again. Maybe we'd have to get an answering machine if this kept up. I knew just what kind of message I'd like to leave on it. "Hello,

I'm not able to come to the phone right now. I'm feeding my cockroaches. Please leave your name and number and I'll get back to you."

I dashed back up the stairs and breathlessly answered, "McIntire residence, Joshua speaking." I must have known it would be Mom calling to check on me. She was impressed with my phone manners. As a secretary she was always telling me how important they were.

"Why are you out of breath, Joshua?" she asked.

"I started my cockroach project, and I've been down in the basement collecting them."

"Oh, Joshua, are you really going to do that? Once the exterminator comes, I never want to see another cockroach."

"Mom, you already said I could. Besides, I'll keep them in my own room in the fruit jars."

"What fruit jars?" Her voice was on edge.

"The ones in the pantry," I replied.

"You didn't use my good fruit jars for those disgusting cockroaches? I can't believe you did that without asking me." She sounded almost hysterical.

I tried to smooth over this tactical error and apologized profusely. "I'm sorry, Mom. I should have asked. But you're never going to use them anyhow."

Now I'd really put my foot in my mouth. I could hear the catch in her voice as she answered.

"Joshua, you don't know that. I might have a

chance next summer. My other line is ringing. Just make sure you wash your hands really well after you're done. We'll talk about this later."

While I was washing up, the phone rang again. I'd heard from everybody important in my life but Dad. Unfortunately the voice on the other end had a higher pitch. Wendell again. When was he going to get the message? I wasn't interested in talking to him, seeing him, or hearing about him.

He was his same obnoxious, cheery self. "I'm calling to see if you want to come over and do homework with me tonight," he offered. This was Wendell's idea of a good time?

"Thanks, but I can't go anywhere unless I check with my mom first, and she's not home." I was getting better with the excuses. This one rolled from the tip of my tongue.

"Well, I'll try again some other time," Wendell said. He didn't sound the least bit hurt or offended. He just didn't get it.

I decided to use the time before Mom came home to observe the cockroaches and take some notes, but I suddenly remembered something really important. I'd screwed the metal lids on the jars. The cockroaches weren't going to live beyond dinner if I didn't get them some air. My *Blatella germanica* were probably suffocating at this very minute.

I took the stairs two at a time, but I'd underesti-

43

mated the heartiness of this breed. They were still furiously crawling around the sides of the jars, looking for a way to escape. Thank goodness the former tenant had left an ample supply of rusty tools in the garage. I found a hammer and screwdriver and proceeded to ventilate my four cockroach motels.

I carried them carefully to my bedroom, spread out my books and papers, and tried to look like a scientist. The most interesting book had lots of colored pictures and drawings. All the body parts were enlarged. I turned to the chapter on how to take care of cockroaches and read it.

Feed your cockroaches dry dog food and slices of apple, potatoes, and carrots. They also need fresh water. One way of providing it is to fill a test tube with water and cap it with a piece of wet cotton.

The other book I'd checked out suggested a more interesting menu—sugary cinnamon rolls and boiled potatoes. But even though I wasn't going to keep them very long, I decided I'd better keep them healthy. Apples and carrots were better than cinnamon rolls. I peeled one of each, sliced them up, and put the slices in the jars. I was beginning to be sorry that I'd collected these creatures for another purpose than observation.

I heard the front door open, and suddenly I remembered two pressing problems. Ben was coming over after dinner, and I'd used the fruit jars without

44

permission. I needed to do some fast talking immediately.

"Mom, I was just about to set the table for dinner. What are we having?" My voice sounded fake even to me.

She looked suspiciously at me, but was too tired to question my motives. "We're having macaroni and cheese, and you can get the water boiling. Have you washed your hands? "

I assured her I was germ-free. While I got the kettle from under the stove, I tried to think of a clever way to get permission for something I'd already made plans to do. "Mom, one of the guys from school wants to come over to work on science projects tonight. Is that okay?"

"Who might that be?" she asked.

"Ben."

"Isn't he the boy that called the other night? I guess it's all right."

I breathed a mental sigh of relief. Now I'd have to call Ben and tell him it was okay for him to come, when he already thought it was okay for him to come. Stretching the truth can sure get complicated.

Ben arrived on the dot of six-thirty. I introduced him to Mom, and he was charming and polite. He looked her right in the eye when he was talking. Mom was always impressed by somebody who could do that.

We went to my bedroom, and Ben was immediately captivated by the cockroaches.

"These are so cool," he gushed. "This is going to be the best thing that anybody ever did at Jefferson School. We are going to blow their minds." His voice was getting louder with each succeeding sentence, and I put my finger to my lips.

"Shhh, I don't want my mom to find out about this. She thinks I'm using these for my science project."

Ben gave me a knowing look and lowered his voice. "When will we be ready to do this?" he wanted to know. "I can hardly wait."

"Just give me a chance to finish my science report, and then we'll do it."

Ben's enthusiasm was contagious. I could just envision the expression on Mrs. Bannister's face. She'd never know who did it, either.

Ben left, and I took one last look at the cockroaches. They hadn't eaten any of the food, but I wasn't worried. They only eat when it's dark. Before I went to bed, I put some pieces of cardboard in each of the jars. One of the books said they like places to hide.

I drifted off to sleep thinking about my dad, the cockroaches, and, strangely enough, Wendell. Wasn't he ever going to give up and stop calling me?

I spent every spare minute that weekend playing with my cockroaches. They reminded me of knights in armor, so I named the two biggest ones King Arthur and Sir Lancelot. I tried one of the experiments suggested in the book. I mixed a little honey with water and smeared it all over Sir Lancelot with a paintbrush. He immediately started giving himself a bath. By the time he was finished, he was cleaner than I was.

I wanted to get a closer look at King Arthur, so on Tuesday I borrowed a magnifying glass from the science lab at school. Mrs. Bannister had seemed very impressed with my eagerness to use scientific equipment. If only she knew the real story.

Every time I tried to get King Arthur to hold still, he scuttled off in a different direction, so one afternoon I tried the book's suggestion of putting him in the refrigerator for ten minutes. If Mom knew, she'd have a conniption, but I did put him in a plastic baggie with a twist tie, just to be safe. He was out cold (in more ways than one) when I checked. I laid him out on a Kleenex.

Is this what doctors feel like when their patients are under anesthesia? I wondered. King Arthur was on his back, and I could see all of the little parts that were described in the encyclopedia article. I sure hoped he would wake up from this deep sleep when his physical was over.

I heard Mom in the driveway and quickly began putting my stuff away. Spying the jars under my arm, she pleaded, "When are we going to get rid of those disgusting bugs?"

Her question reminded me that Ben was also pressuring me to finish my assignment. I hadn't counted on getting so involved in the subject. I decided to write the final draft of my report tonight so we could get it over with. I took the cockroaches back to my bedroom and watched as King Arthur slowly began to wave his antennae. He gained speed and I relaxed. He was going to be okay.

While Mom and I were eating our submarine sandwiches, the phone rang.

She answered it. "Oh, hello, Wendell. How are you? Joshua? He's right here."

I was cornered. I had no choice but to take the call. I already knew what he was going to say. It was his church club night again.

"Hi, Wendell." I listened. "Thanks for asking, but I've got to write my science report tonight."

My mom was making funny faces and waving her hands.

I paused. "Just a minute, Wendell." I held my hand over the mouthpiece. "What's the matter, Mom?"

"Is Wendell asking you to his group at church?"

How did she know?

"Yeah, but I can't go. I have to write my science report."

She gave me a stern look. "When is it due, Joshua? Tell me the truth."

"Next Monday," I confessed.

"Well then," she said brightly, "there's no reason you can't go with Wendell tonight. You've spent far too much time with those repulsive cockroaches anyhow." She motioned for me to put the phone back to my ear. "Tell him you'll go, Joshua."

I was trapped. The only other solution involved an argument, and I couldn't afford to have Mom mad at me right now.

"Okay, Wendell," I moaned into the phone. Maybe I could get sick in the next hour.

Wendell seemed oblivious to the dilemma he had created. In his most annoyingly cheerful tone, he promised to pick me up at 6:45. I hoped we wouldn't see anyone I knew.

True to his word, Wendell rang the doorbell promptly at a quarter to seven. Mom invited him in.

"Hi, Wendell. How are you?" She was really laying it on.

"Fine, thank you, Mrs. McIntire." Wendell was playing the game.

"Has Joshua told you about the cockroach experiment he's doing for science?"

Wendell looked at me with surprise. "Uh, no, Mrs. McIntire. He hasn't."

"Well, Joshua, take Wendell into your bedroom and show him what you've been doing." Suddenly she was in love with my cockroaches. Grown-ups are too much.

I reluctantly led Wendell into my room. He knelt down in front of the desk and watched Sir Lancelot and King Arthur. They were pretty lazy after all the exercise we'd had after school.

"These are neat. Are you really doing your science report on them?" Wendell asked.

I nodded.

"Have they fought over their food yet? I read once that they're pretty aggressive animals when they're hungry."

For a minute I forgot who I was talking to and began to describe the confrontation between Sir Lancelot and a smaller cockroach the day before. Wendell told me he'd once seen a television program where they showed cockroaches fighting in slow motion.

"Boys," my mom called. "You're going to be late if you don't get started."

I looked at Wendell as we walked out of the bedroom and realized that I hadn't even thought about what he was wearing while we were talking about cockroaches.

The Grandville Community Church was only a few blocks away. We walked down the narrow sidewalk shoulder to shoulder, still talking about cockroaches.

"Does Mrs. Bannister know what you're doing your report on?" Wendell asked.

"No, I haven't said anything." I felt very uncomfortable. Wendell was asking questions that were none of his business. Fortunately we got to the church, and that ended the discussion.

I hadn't been to church more than three or four times in my whole life. The last time was when my Aunt Kathy got married. All I could remember was the stained glass windows and the flower girl who cried all the way down the aisle.

Wendell's church wasn't nearly as fancy. There wasn't any stained glass, but they did have a gym. What could a church possibly want with a gym? I thought people went to church to sit in pews and hear sermons.

Wendell was obviously at home here. No one seemed to care about what he was wearing. His outfit tonight was another winner. Navy blue polyester pants and a shirt that looked like some first grader had thrown up on it. To finish off the outfit, he was wearing a ridiculous gray and red vest with badges sewn all over it. Where did he find these clothes?

A bulky man with his stomach spilling out of a gray and red uniform came over to say hello. And right behind him was a familiar face. (Could I just pretend I wasn't there? Maybe the floor would open up and swallow me.) It was Tracy Kendall, the redhead from school. Wendell hadn't told me she went to his church.

"Hi, Wendell. Hi, Joshua. I didn't know you were coming to Awana." Tracy's greeting was normal enough, but she lingered over the word you. She seemed to accept the fact that I was with Wendell as perfectly normal. "Wanna shoot some baskets?"

The gym was filling up with kids of all shapes and sizes, and the noise level reminded me of a carnival.

Before we had time to get started, the whistle blew and club began. It went nonstop. We had a four-way tug-o-war, a bean bag toss, and some running relays. There was no way I would get away with running water over my hair after this workout. I'd need a shower for sure.

Then I listened to Wendell and Tracy recite their memory work for Mrs. Stehouwer, one of the leaders. They were awesome. I couldn't believe they knew this stuff by heart. I didn't really understand it all, but one of the verses stuck in my mind. It talked about God being our Heavenly Father and looking out for us all the time. I'd have to ask Wendell about it later. My father on earth wasn't doing such a hot job. I guessed I could use one in heaven.

After the memory work, somebody rolled in a big screen TV, and the leader popped a cassette in the recorder. I couldn't believe we were going to watch a video at church. Maybe I'd come again after all. It was a cartoon about a character named McGee, and he was trying to convince this other kid that it was better to be last than first. Obviously McGee had never had to eat what was left in the lunchroom if you were last in line. But the way McGee told the story, I could see his point.

When we'd had our refreshments, Tracy came over to say goodbye and said she'd see me in class the next day. She invited me to come back next week. I told her I'd think about it. I wasn't sure I could handle Wendell that often.

We were quiet on the way home. I was tired from playing all of the games, and I couldn't sort out how I felt about everything that was happening to me. Right now it seemed that I didn't have control of anything. My dad hadn't called yet. I was right in the middle of this cockroach project, and Wendell kept complicating things by inviting me to church. I just wanted to be left alone.

That night as I lay in bed, the words that Wendell had recited at Awana came back to me. I thought about having another father in heaven, and I felt strangely calm. It was the last thing I thought of before falling asleep.

When I got to school in the morning, Ben cornered me as I locked my bike in the rack.

"We've got to do this cockroach thing tomorrow, Joshua. I am so totally bored right now. The only interesting thing that's happened this week was the false fire alarm."

I wasn't up to pressure from Ben today. I didn't know what I wanted to do.

"You're not chickening out, are you?" he demanded.

"Nah," I said. "I'm just tired."

"Well, I hope not. This is really a big deal. We're going to go down in history at Jefferson School."

I was cornered. I didn't dare let Ben know that I was having second thoughts. The last thing I needed was to have him think I was a wimp.

Grudgingly I agreed to meet him early tomorrow

morning near the bike rack. I would have the cockroaches ready to go.

When I got home from school, I couldn't eat anything. I sat on my bed staring at the cockroaches. They were quiet now, but if I moved the glass jars, Sir Lancelot and King Arthur would wave their antennae at me eagerly. What was I going to do? If I didn't show up with the cockroaches, my name would be mud. Ben was my only real friend at Jefferson, and I'd promised him I would do something. If I broke that promise, what kind of friend was I?

I made up my mind. The cockroaches would go to school tomorrow—at least all of them but King Arthur and Sir Lancelot. I couldn't part with them.

Mom came home and fixed my favorite dinner, pizza bagels, but I only ate one.

"What's the matter, Joshua? Are you sick?"

Mom always knew when something was bothering me. But I couldn't talk to her about this one. I knew what she'd say, and I didn't want to hear it.

I tried to watch my favorite TV show, but I couldn't concentrate. When the phone rang, I ran to get it. Maybe it was Ben telling me he'd changed his mind.

But the voice on the other end was deep. For a minute I didn't even recognize it.

"Hi, Joshua. Remember me?" It was Dad, trying to be humorous. He never was very good at jokes. "I guess you've been wondering what happened to me."

That was the understatement of the century, but I was too nervous to say much. Now that I had him on the phone, I didn't want to sound stupid. "Are you okay, Dad?" I asked.

"I'm really sorry I haven't called, Joshua, but things have been up in the air. I've been looking for a new job, and I just haven't had much time."

The excuses didn't quite sound right, but I didn't argue. After all, he was still my dad.

"So, how's the new school? Have you made any friends yet?" he asked.

He sure knew how to get right to the difficult subjects. "I'm doing fine, Dad. I've got loads of friends."

"Well, that's great, Joshua. I knew you wouldn't have any trouble adjusting." He sounded far away and out of touch. I didn't know what else to say.

"How's your mom doing?"

He had a lot of nerve asking about her. He was the one who left home. I couldn't keep the anger out of my voice. "So, why do you want to know, Dad?"

"Sorry, Joshua. I should ask her that question. Well, I've got to go. I have to meet someone for dinner. I'll call again soon. Bye."

"Bye, Dad." His voice was gone, and I stared at the phone in my hand. Mom had her back to me across the room. We didn't say anything. I just walked to my bedroom and shut the door.

I set my alarm for early the next morning. I needed extra time to get the cockroaches together for their trip to Jefferson. I tossed and turned all night long and finally fell asleep just when the sky was beginning to lighten. When the alarm rang, I was groggy—then I suddenly remembered what was in store. I pulled the covers over my head and tried to decide if I could be sick. But Project Cockroach had great possibilities. I could be the hero of 5B if I just didn't chicken out.

I brushed my teeth, threw some water on my hair so it would look like I'd showered, and put on my Jefferson Jaguars shirt. This was going to be an interesting day.

The sleeping cockroaches had no idea what was in store for them. I found a box in the closet and emptied all of them except Arthur and Lancelot into it. They were mad about being waked up.

Mom was already in the kitchen. "What are you doing up at this hour, Joshua?"

"I'm getting the cockroaches ready to take to school. I'm showing them to the class today." That was stretching it a bit. But the class certainly would be seeing them at some point.

"Well, thank goodness, they'll be gone for good," she said.

I didn't know how to tell her about Lancelot and Arthur.

"I'm leaving a little early so I can get them into class before school starts." Another slight stretch of the truth.

"Joshua, I'm really impressed by how hard you've worked on this project. I certainly hope you get an A. You deserve it." She smiled broadly and squeezed my shoulder.

I finished up my scrambled eggs, grabbed my jacket and the cockroach box, and was out the door. I decided not to risk riding my bike. I didn't want to balance the cockroach box and shift gears at the same time.

Ben was already in front of school when I got there. We walked up the hill toward the playground and sat on the railroad ties that surrounded the equipment. "Let me see them," said Ben. I opened the box, and the cockroaches swarmed angrily around. They had become accustomed to our routine and weren't happy about the change.

Ben pulled a smaller box out of his back pack. "Look what I found at home." It was a box from Scheffler's Florist Shop. "My sister got a corsage from her boyfriend in this. It'll be perfect to disguise the cockroaches."

I had to admit Ben was pretty smart.

We walked to the front door, the only one open this early. Only the teachers were supposed to be in the building. I hoped nobody would notice us wandering around, or our plan could go down the drain before we started.

"Just let me do all of the talking, Joshua. I know the teachers around here."

I was sure that the teachers all knew Ben, too. Maybe this wasn't such a good idea after all.

Surprisingly enough, we only ran into the custodian, Mr. Brown.

"What are you boys doing in here so early? Oh, I see, you've got a surprise for your teacher. Well, I won't tell her I saw you."

The classroom door was already opened, and we quickly made our way to Mrs. Bannister's desk. I had butterflies in my stomach . . . or should I say cockroaches? Ben opened the desk drawer and quickly emptied the box. The cockroaches spilled out and scurried over the paper clips and Post-It notes. There was no turning back now.

When the bell rang, the kids from 5B lined up in our usual spot. Suddenly I was more aware than ever of Mrs. Bannister. She had a funny expression on her face and was biting her lip. I wondered if she'd already found the cockroaches.

Everybody went into the building laughing and talking. Ben was poking Tracy and teasing her about her red hair. I wondered how he could be so relaxed. My stomach felt sick, just as it had on the first day of school. The suspense was unbearable.

Mrs. Bannister took attendance and handed out lunch tickets. Today was pizza day, and just about everybody was having hot lunch.

"Class, today we're going to do something different. We'll be rearranging our desks and working in cooperative groups."

Cooperative groups sounded suspiciously like working with people you didn't like.

Mrs. Bannister continued. "I've put each of you

in a group of four. You'll be working as a team and competing for points."

My ears perked up when I heard the word competition. Maybe this would be fun. For just a second I forgot about Project Cockroach.

Mrs. Bannister read off names from her clipboard. "Joshua, you're over here with Wendell, Tracy, and Sondra."

I couldn't believe my luck. Tracy and Sondra weren't too bad, although Sondra was a bit of a whiner, but Wendell. . . . Our group would never win anything with Wendell.

Our square of desks was up front near Mrs. Bannister's. If I'd had x-ray vision, I could have seen the cockroaches.

"Listen up, class. The purpose of this exercise is to teach you interdependence." I didn't know what that word meant, but Mrs. Bannister explained.

"Interdependence means depending on someone else for help. Most of the time I ask you to do your work alone. But—" Tracy was waving her hand in the air.

"What is it, Tracy?" Mrs. Bannister asked.

"Isn't that cheating?"

"Not when you're working in cooperative groups," Mrs. Bannister replied. "When you cooperate, you can do things together you could never accomplish alone."

I thought of the cockroaches again. It was a cinch I'd never have done that one by myself.

Mrs. Bannister was walking toward her desk. My heart began to pound. Then she suddenly veered off toward the big cupboard. She was looking for something. "Has anyone seen my masking tape?" She glanced around the room and then walked back toward her desk. The pounding in my chest got louder. I was sure everyone in the room could hear it. She opened the cockroach drawer.

The next moment will be frozen in my mind forever. Mrs. Bannister screamed. It wasn't a little shriek or a squeal, but a major fifteen second, panic-stricken howl. She sounded genuinely terrified. Everyone in the class was stunned speechless.

Once she got the scream out, Mrs. Bannister acted perfectly normal again. Even though Mrs. Heaton from across the hall and Mr. Truitt from next door came running, it was Mrs. Bannister who was calm.

"This is simply intolerable. I will not have bugs in my desk. Mr. Truitt, get the custodian."

Mrs. Bannister pushed the intercom button and called the office. "Miss Lincoln, we have an emergency in 5B. Could you please send the principal?"

Nobody was laughing this time. They were thinking what I was thinking. How could anyone have played such a horrible trick on Mrs. Bannister?

Mr. Brown arrived with a garbage pail on wheels. Mrs. Bannister brushed him aside and dumped the entire drawer into the pail. It made a loud noise when it hit bottom. I cringed to think of my cockroaches, crushed underneath everything. "Take it away," she ordered.

Mrs. Raymond, the principal, took Mrs. Bannister out in the hall. All I could see was the gaping hole where the drawer had been. Everybody was talking to each other now. Wendell turned to me and whispered, "I'll bet I know who did that." I felt sick.

Mrs. Raymond and Mrs. Bannister came back into the classroom. Then the principal took Steve Adamson out of the room with her. I couldn't figure out what was going on. Mrs. Bannister kept on teaching as if nothing had happened. Steve came back and sent Tracy to the office.

Now I got the picture. The principal was interrogating our class. I wondered if she used torture to get the truth out of her suspects. Suddenly all of the promises I'd made my mom about having a good school year were going down the tubes. Wendell hadn't been to the office yet, but it was only a matter of time. Mario tapped me on the shoulder. "It's your turn," he muttered.

I felt like I had lead in both of my shoes. I passed the doors to the playground and thought about running away. Maybe I could call Dad. But I didn't

64

know his number. The secretary outside Mrs. Raymond's office gave me a big smile. "Hi, Joshua, go right on in." What right did she have to be so cheerful?

I'd never been in Mrs. Raymond's office before. She was talking on the phone, and I nervously looked at her bulletin board. It was crammed full of junk—yellowed newspaper clippings, silly buttons, and snapshots of her in a Halloween costume. I wished I had more time to look at everything, but she was off the phone and sitting down at the table next to me.

"Good morning, Joshua. I just want to ask you a few questions about the cockroaches in Mrs. Bannister's desk. Do you know who put them there?" She certainly got right to the point.

"I have a feeling you know something about this, Joshua," she continued. "Why don't you tell me about it?"

"What do you mean?" I asked. I could feel the silly grin I always get when I'm nervous spreading over my face. But inside I wasn't grinning.

"This isn't funny, Joshua. Mr. Brown saw two boys in the hallway before school this morning. He's pretty sure they were you and Ben."

"I was just bringing in some stuff for my science report," I said.

"I think you were bringing in more than just a

report," said Mrs. Raymond. "I think you brought in those cockroaches." She didn't raise her voice, and somehow that made me feel even worse. "Why don't you just tell me the truth?"

All of a sudden the grin vanished, and tears started to well up in my eyes. Oh, no. On top of everything else, I was going to cry. Now my eyes would be all red and puffy. At that thought, I really started blubbering.

Mrs. Raymond put her hand on my shoulder. "Joshua, everybody makes mistakes. Nobody's perfect. The important thing is how you handle your mistakes and what you learn from them."

She grabbed a Kleenex from on top of her desk and pushed it toward me. "I need to have a straight answer, Joshua. Did the cockroaches belong to you?"

I nodded.

"Do you know why Mrs. Bannister feels the way she does about bugs?"

"No," I answered faintly.

"Because she is allergic to them. She gets very ill when she's around insects."

Mrs. Raymond was being so nice. I began to feel a little better. But then she lowered the boom. "Joshua, we're going to call your mother now and tell her about this. You and Ben will be serving after-school detentions for several weeks to pay for this prank."

I sniffled a little into my tissue. This was the

worst day of my life. "Can't I just serve the detentions without telling my mother?"

Mrs. Raymond smiled faintly. "Joshua, I want this experience to be as painful as possible so that you'll never be back here again. That's why we're calling your mother."

She reached for the phone. In my mind I could see my mother sitting at her desk. She had left that morning thinking I was going off to get an A in science. Now she'd be getting a call about some stupid trick I'd pulled. Why was I so dumb?

Then there was Ben. No matter what I said, he'd think I ratted. And Mrs. Bannister. She'd never trust me again.

Mrs. Raymond interrupted my thoughts. "Joshua, there's something else we have to do after we call your mother. Do you know what that might be?" She gave me the answer. "You'll have to apologize to Mrs. Bannister and ask her to forgive you."

I groaned inwardly. Mrs. Raymond must have known how I felt.

"That will be almost as hard as telling your mom, Joshua. But it has to be done if you and Mrs. Bannister are going to work together this year."

I couldn't imagine Mrs. Raymond having to ask anyone for forgiveness, but she sounded as though she'd done it once or twice.

All of a sudden I felt strangely lighthearted. I

wondered if I was getting sick. I'd just gotten caught playing the worst trick ever, and I felt good. Maybe Mrs. Raymond knew something about forgiveness that I didn't know.

I got back to class just as the lunch bell rang. Mrs. Bannister asked if she could talk to me for a couple of minutes. It was now or never.

We looked at each other for a second. "Is there something you want to say to me, Joshua?"

"I'm really sorry about the cockroaches, Mrs. Bannister." I wanted to tell her that if I'd known about her allergies I never would have done anything so stupid, but I couldn't quite get out the words. "I won't ever do anything dumb like that again."

"There's nothing harder than saying you're sorry, Joshua. I hope that we can forget about this and work together this year."

"There is one thing, Mrs. Bannister." I had to say it. "I really am doing my science project on cockroaches. Does this mean I have to start over?"

"Joshua, you can do your project on anything you want to. All I ask is that you keep the bugs in *your* desk." She had a somber look on her face, but there was a twinkle in her eye. Maybe there was hope after all.

Talking with Mrs. Bannister had made me late for lunch. I hoped they wouldn't run out of pizza. Then my day really would be ruined. At the lunch table, everybody seemed to be more interested in eating than in talking, and I was glad that the subject of cockroaches didn't come up.

I wasn't sure that Mom was going to be so understanding. Her car was already in the driveway when I got home—not a good sign. She was sitting at the kitchen table with a cup of tea. She always drinks tea when she's upset. She looked like she'd been crying.

I stood and looked at her for a minute, and then I couldn't help myself. I ran over and hugged her.

"Joshua, don't think you can pay for this incident with a little hug. I'm really upset." Her eyes narrowed, and she got that sharp tone to her voice. "You're grounded for the next two weeks."

Inwardly I sighed. Now that I knew what the punishment was, I could handle it.

"You can go only two places," she added. "School and church."

I couldn't believe what I was hearing. She was sending me to church.

"You don't have enough positive influences in

your life. I've decided we're going to change that starting this Sunday."

"Aw, Mom, are you serious?" I groaned.

"Joshua, don't you dare get smart with me, or you'll be grounded for another two weeks. We're going to church Sunday with Wendell and his family."

It wasn't bad enough that we were going to church—we had to go with the Hathaways. I hadn't met Wendell's parents yet, but anybody who let Wendell out of the house wearing those weird outfits had to be pretty strange.

Lancelot and Arthur were in their fruit jar. The other jars stood empty on my desk—grim reminders of Project Cockroach. Ben had been called to the office during lunch. He was probably mad at me. I'd really blown it.

"Lancelot," I said. "Where did I mess up?"

The cockroach waved his antennae at me as if to say, "You'll survive."

That's easy for you to say, I thought.

Since I was stuck at home for two weeks, I figured I might as well make good use of my time. I'd start by writing up my science project. I'd really need a great report to get back in Mrs. Bannister's good graces.

Then I realized I'd forgotten the assignment

sheet she gave us. It occurred to me that I could call Wendell. Nah, why would I want to do that? But I needed that sheet now.

"Mom," I called. "Can I make a phone call?"

"It depends on whom you're going to call. If it's Ben Anderson, forget it. He's off limits for awhile."

"I want to call Wendell," I said. "I need the directions for our science report."

"In that case," she replied, "it's okay."

This was certainly a first. Me calling Wendell. He would probably fall off his chair.

But Wendell didn't sound at all surprised when he answered the phone. It was like he knew I would call sooner or later.

"Wendell, could I borrow your science report directions?"

"Sure," he said. "When do you wanna get them?"

"Uh, I can't," I mumbled. "I'm, uh, grounded for awhile."

"Oh," said Wendell. "I guess you got in a lot of trouble over the cockroaches." He didn't sound like he was gloating or anything, and I appreciated that.

"I could bring it over," he offered.

Suddenly I was looking forward to seeing Wendell, although I couldn't really figure out why. I guess when you're grounded, anybody looks good.

It was the weekend before I knew it. Between finishing my science report and doing all of the other homework Mrs. Bannister assigned, I didn't have much time to be depressed. Besides, Wendell came over a couple of times, and we did some more experiments with the cockroaches. It was his idea to see if Lancelot and Arthur could swim. He'd read somewhere that cockroaches can get into people's houses through the sewer pipes. We filled a pail with water and watched them swim happily around.

On Saturday night Mom reminded me that we were going to church in the morning. She dug out a tie I'd worn to my aunt's wedding. It was the clip-on kind and a little short, but she insisted. I was making a Wendell Hathaway fashion statement.

We rode to church with the Hathaways. It was the first time I'd met Wendell's family, and they looked surprisingly normal. I wondered if Wendell was adopted.

I don't know what I was expecting, but I was sure surprised. Church wasn't stuffy and boring. There was lots of great music with amplifiers and a guitar. The minister even made some jokes. I wasn't sure I understood everything he was saying, but I passed the time by counting the flakes of dandruff on the shoulders of the man in front of me. I got up to 297 before the sermon caught my attention.

The minister was talking about Jesus feeding five

thousand people with a few pieces of bread and fish. Some magic act! I'd heard of Jesus before, of course. The minister said Jesus was the Son of God. But I didn't quite have it figured out how He'd gotten down from heaven where God was supposed to be. Nobody else looked confused.

After church, the Hathaways invited us over for Sunday dinner. We never eat Sunday dinner at our house. I mean, of course we eat on Sundays, but not like they do at the Hathaways. Mrs. Hathaway had a pot roast, mashed potatoes, and what seemed like six different vegetables. Every time the vegetables came around, I passed them on to Wendell's little sister. She wasn't taking any, either.

My mom and the Hathaways talked about grown-up things, and Wendell and I just ate. I didn't feel as awkward as I used to around him, and sometimes I even forgot to notice what he was wearing. After homemade apple pie for dessert, Wendell took me up to his bedroom. When he opened the door, a light came on and a buzzer rang.

"What's that?" I asked.

"Oh, I made that out of a Radio Shack kit I got for Christmas," explained Wendell. "It keeps my sister from snooping in my room."

I didn't have to worry about any snooping sisters.

Wendell's room wasn't at all what I expected. It was really pretty messy. He had lots of books, and I also noticed a leather-bound Bible on his nightstand.

"Remember that stuff you were reciting at Awana the other night?" I asked.

"Which stuff?" asked Wendell.

"The stuff about God being our Father in heaven and watching out for us," I said.

"Oh, that's Matthew 6," said Wendell. "Do you want to read it for yourself?"

I got embarrassed and shrugged my shoulders.

"Here," he said. "It's right here." Wendell flipped right to the spot and began reading aloud. Now I really was embarrassed. If anybody in my old school saw me, they'd be laughing for sure.

" 'So don't worry at all about having enough food and clothing. . . . Your heavenly Father already knows perfectly well that you need them, and He will give them to you if you give Him first place in your life and live as He wants you to,' " Wendell read. "Do you know what that means?" he asked.

"I'm not sure," I said.

"That you never need to worry about anything, if you trust in God."

I wondered for a minute if God could bring my mom and dad back together again. That was my biggest worry right now. But I didn't want to talk to Wendell about that.

"Come on, Wendell. Let's go back downstairs."

Wendell didn't argue.

75

Wendell and I were walking to school together every day now. I'm not sure how it happened, but he started stopping by and I was usually waiting. We took the tunnel. I still didn't like to be down there, even with somebody else. It smelled like a refrigerator that needed cleaning.

Wendell and I had just rounded the first corner when a dark figure jumped into our pathway. It was only Ben Anderson, but both of us jumped a mile.

"Hi, guys," Ben said.

"How come you did that?" I asked.

"Just wanted to see if you and Weird Wendell here could take care of yourselves. Lots of strange things happen to kids in this tunnel." Ben's voice sounded threatening. "Isn't that right, Wendell?" he continued. Ben gave Wendell's arm a little punch to accentuate each word.

Wendell just stood there. I didn't say a word. This was the first time Ben had spoken to me since the cockroach incident. Wendell gave me a funny look as Ben ran off toward school.

"What do you suppose he's up to?" I asked Wendell.

"Trouble," said Wendell.

But Ben made it a point to be nice to me all day. He picked me for his team in gym and saved a seat for me at lunch. Maybe we could be friends after all.

I had asked Mom at breakfast if I could go to town after school. It was the first day of my "freedom," and I was anxious to get back to Main Street to see if the leather coat was still there. Wendell was staying to work in the computer lab, and that was fine with me. He was so good, he got on my nerves sometimes.

I saw Ben up ahead and called to him. "Hey, wanna go to town with me?"

"Sure, where you goin'?" Ben wanted to know.

"Just around," I answered, not wanting to tell Ben about the coat.

"Hey, Joshua, you're not still mad about that little cockroach thing, are you?" Ben asked.

"Nah, it's over," I said. "I just don't want to do anything that dumb again."

"My dad thought it was a great trick," said Ben. "He laughed all night long. Said he wished he'd thought of it."

That's not what my dad would have said.

"Hey," said Ben, "let's go up on the train tracks and fool around."

I wasn't sure. The last time I'd listened to Ben had ended in disaster.

"Come on, Josh. This isn't like the cockroach thing. Nothing can happen on the train tracks." Ben was very persuasive.

I had to admit the tracks were impressive. With the steep embankments on either side, walking them was like balancing on a tightrope. We kept going until we came to LaVeen's Lumber and Material Company.

Looking down into the lumber yard was neat. There were big concrete bins filled with different colored stones and gravel. I was about to jump into the bin filled with sand, when a workman driving a front loader waved and yelled to us.

"Hey, you boys better get off those tracks. The 4:45 will be coming through soon."

"Yikes!" I shouted. "I'm going to be late for dinner. Let's get going."

We ran down the tracks toward town. I don't remember how it happened, but the next thing I knew I was rolling down the embankment. I landed in the brush at the bottom and looked up to see Ben laughing his head off.

"Boy, did you look great going down that hill! You could be a stunt man in the movies!"

I tried moving my leg. "I don't feel like a stunt man in the movies. They always get up and run away."

Ben looked alarmed. "What do you mean? Come on, let's get going."

"I'm serious, Ben. I can't move my leg. It hurts really bad." I wasn't crying, but I sure wanted to.

"Well, what are you going to do?" Ben asked.

"I'm not going to do anything. You gotta get me some help."

"We're really going to get it," said Ben. "We're not supposed to be playing on these tracks. The railroad police have already given me one warning. I've gotta get out of here."

"But you can't just leave me," I said.

"I'll send somebody to help you." Ben turned and ran.

I tried calling for help, but no one came. I knew what time it was, though—the 4:45 was coming down the tracks. I'd never been that close to a train before. The ground shook as it passed by, and I had to cover my ears. I could see the commuters behind the train windows, but nobody noticed me.

I tried to drag myself along, but sharp pains shot through my leg. One of them nearly took my breath away. I decided I'd better wait for help . . . that is, if help would ever come.

I read somewhere that when people are about to

die, their whole life flashes in front of them. I didn't think I was dying, but the whole day did flash in front of me. Boy, had I made some major mistakes.

Mistake Number One was not punching Ben Anderson in the nose when he roughed up Wendell in the tunnel this morning. Mistake Number Two was not telling Ben Anderson what a crummy idea playing on the train tracks was. Was I dumb or what? Why did I always have to figure things out when it was too late to fix them?

I don't know how long I lay in the brush, but it felt like forever. I'd read books about people surviving in the wilderness, but they didn't have broken legs, and I was pretty sure that's what I had.

I tried crying for help again. After the third try, I thought I heard someone answer. I called again, and then I heard it more clearly. A voice from down the tracks was calling, "I'm coming, Joshua. Just wait."

This was no time for jokes. I wasn't going anywhere. The voice was getting closer, and now I recognized it. It belonged to Wendell Hathaway, Worst Dressed Fifth Grader in the World. But at that moment I didn't care what Wendell was wearing. I just wanted to get home.

Wendell made his way carefully down the hill, starting a mini-avalanche of gravel. He stood for a moment and stared at me. I couldn't tell what he was thinking.

"How'd you know I was here?" I asked.

"I ran into Ben when I was walking home from school. He told me what happened, so I came looking for you. Do you think you can walk if I help you?"

"I'm not sure," I said. "I don't think so. What are we going to do?"

"Don't worry," said Wendell. "I know exactly what to do. I did a badge in Awana on First Aid and Safety. You need the paramedics."

I groaned. "I was hoping I could sort of sneak into the house and pretend nothing happened."

"Don't be stupid," Wendell said. Wendell wasn't usually that harsh. "You'll have to wait here until I can get help," he went on. "I'm going to run over to the fire department."

Suddenly I was glad to let Wendell take over all of the decision making. He ran off down the tracks, and I closed my eyes and drifted off. The next thing I knew, there was Wendell with two paramedics and a stretcher. I had no idea where they'd come from, but I was sure glad to see them.

They took out a big pair of scissors and cut away the leg of my new jeans. My mom was going to be mad. My leg looked sort of bent and funny. It was all swollen and starting to turn purple. I thought I was going to throw up. "What's your name?" the man with the mustache asked.

"Joshua McIntire," I answered.

He turned to Wendell and asked, "Were you here when this happened?"

"It's kind of complicated," I said.

"Well, we can get it all sorted out at the hospital," he said.

I wasn't sure I'd heard him right. "Did you say hospital?"

"Where did you think you were going to get this leg set, at the grocery store?" the other paramedic joked.

I didn't think he was very funny, but his partner gave a big guffaw.

They put me on the stretcher and carried me off. The closest road was about half a mile away, but they'd driven the ambulance right through an open field next to the tracks. I was glad I didn't have to ride the stretcher much further. My leg was really beginning to throb.

Wendell walked alongside and kept his hand on the stretcher. I wondered how he'd learned to be so thoughtful.

It wasn't far to Westfield Community Hospital. Wendell rode with me. I was supposed to be home by five o'clock, and my mom was probably having a fit wondering where I was.

We pulled up to the emergency room, and they wheeled me in through the big double doors. If I hadn't felt so rotten, it might have been fun. A nurse with a clipboard started asking me all kinds of questions, like my address and phone number and did my parents have medical insurance.

Right now, all I wanted was to see my mom. I didn't even care if she bawled me out royally. I could hear the nurse on the phone giving her directions for getting to the hospital.

"Don't worry, Mrs. McIntire, he'll be fine. He's conscious, and we won't do a thing until you get here."

There was a thin curtain separating my bed from one a few feet away. I could hear a man wheezing and coughing. He sounded like he might die any minute. I hoped no one died while I was here. Especially not me.

Mom must have broken the speed limit, because she got there right away. "We'll talk about how all of this happened later, Joshua. The important thing is to get you fixed up right away." She had tears in her eyes and she gave me a big hug.

A pretty woman with a stethoscope around her neck came through the curtains. "I'm Dr. Lantinga, Joshua. I want to examine you, and then we'll send you off to x-rays for some pictures. We're going to get some prize-winners by the looks of this leg."

The next hour flew by. I had x-rays, got my broken leg set, and got fitted for crutches.

"Can I walk to school on crutches?" I wondered.

"Probably not, unless it's right across the street," the technician advised.

"How am I going to get there then?" I worried. "Mom leaves for work before I leave for school."

"I've got a great idea," said Wendell. "We've got an old wheelchair that my grandmother uses when she visits."

Mom looked a little skeptical, but Wendell persuaded her. "I'll pick up Josh and deliver him every day. It'll be perfect."

Mom thought for a second and said, "At least I'll know he's in good hands."

She smiled confidently at Wendell.

Wendell arrived early the next morning with my wheelchair. It was a little rusty, but I couldn't complain since I was getting a free ride. Mom said she'd call the school nurse and Mrs. Bannister when she got to work. There were some things I wasn't going to be able to do for quite awhile. But having my own personal chauffeur wasn't half bad.

"Hey, Wendell. You're hitting all the potholes," I complained.

"You're not exactly a lightweight, McIntire," he said.

We hit a level stretch of new sidewalk, and Wendell picked up a little speed. He was jogging behind the chair with a rhythmic step, and I started to chant, "Faster, faster, faster."

But Wendell suddenly stopped running and brought the wheelchair to a stop. "I don't want you to end up with a smashed face along with your broken leg."

I settled back and watched the passing scenery. We took the long way through town, as managing the steps leading down to the tunnel would be impossible. We passed Studebaker's Leather Emporium, and I noticed that the coat was still in the window.

"See that coat?" I asked Wendell.

"What about it?" he responded.

"I'd like to buy it for my mom," I said. "Do you like it?"

"It's not exactly my style," said Wendell.

I chuckled under my breath. Wendell didn't have a style. But somehow, humming along in my wheelchair, I didn't care.

"Have you ever met Mr. Studebaker?" Wendell asked.

"Once, when we first moved to town," I answered.

"He's in a rock band," said Wendell.

"That's not surprising. He looks like a rock star."

"It's a Christian rock band," continued Wendell.

"What's a Christian?" I asked.

"I'm a Christian," said Wendell.

"So that doesn't tell me much." I was doing some fast thinking. I knew two Christians—Wendell and Mr. Studebaker. They both wore unusual clothes.

"Do Christians dress funny?" I asked Wendell.

"It doesn't have anything to do with the way you dress," said Wendell. "It has to do with what you believe and how you act."

We were almost to school, but I wanted to hear more. "Can we talk some more after school?"

"You don't have much choice, McIntire," Wendell laughed. "You're not going home without me."

Jefferson School was built in 1921, before anybody worried about handicapped people using buildings. There was no way I could get my wheelchair up all the stairs and in the door. In fact, we couldn't even get to the playground. The building was built right into the side of a hill, and there were steps everywhere.

"What do you think we should do?" asked Wendell.

"Well, we could get Mr. Brown to help us carry it up," I suggested.

"Let's leave the wheelchair down here in the storeroom," said Wendell. "I'll help you up the stairs."

"But how am I going to get around when I get to the top?" I asked.

"Gosh, this is complicated," said Wendell. "I know. You can use your crutches."

"There's only one problem, Wendell. I left my crutches at home."

"I'll run back and get them," he said. "I'll use the tunnel shortcut. It won't take me long."

"What do I do in the meantime?" I wondered.

"Just sit in your wheelchair and wait for me."

"Great. I'll be the new tourist attraction for everybody that comes by."

Wendell looked at me with a disgusted expression. "I'm trying to help you, Joshua. Quit complaining."

Wendell was right. I was getting a little irritable. I never realized how hard it was to depend on someone else for every move you make.

"Okay," I said, handing him my house key. "I'll be right here when you get back."

I was looking through my homework folder when Mrs. Bannister came along.

"My goodness, Joshua, what happened to you?"

"I broke my leg," I said.

"It looks pretty serious. How long will you be in a wheelchair?"

"I'm not really in a wheelchair," I said. "I've got crutches."

She looked puzzled. "Joshua, I'm a little confused. I do see a wheelchair, but I don't see any crutches."

"Oh." I laughed. "Wendell went back home to get the crutches. We forgot them."

"So Wendell's involved in this, is he?"

The whole story spilled out. "Wendell saved my life. If it hadn't been for him, I'd still be lying by the railroad tracks, probably dead." I wasn't sure if the last part was true, but it sounded good.

"Sounds as if Wendell is a pretty good friend," Mrs. Bannister said. "If you need any help, just holler. Someone will hear you and come running. See you in class."

Two first-grade teachers came by next. They were young and pretty and always together. "Oooh, look what happened to you." First-grade teachers always sound so gushy and sweet. But I didn't mind the attention.

"I've got a broken leg," I said in my best macho manner.

"Oooh, does it hurt?" one of them asked.

I was going to play this for all it was worth. "A little, but I'm doing pretty well."

"Can I autograph your cast for you?" Mrs. Swenson, the blonde one, took out a marker.

How could I refuse? Maybe I'd just sit here all day at the bottom of the stairs and get my cast autographed. While Mrs. Swenson signed her name with a smiley face next to it, Mr. Shonkwiler, a sixth-grade teacher, came wheeling his bike in. He was a long-distance rider and did fifteen miles back and forth to school every day.

"Hey, Joshua. I see I'm not the only one on wheels today."

I liked his sense of humor and wanted to be in his class next year.

He parked his bike in the storeroom and came back to climb the stairs. "A friend at the fire department told me about your accident. You were lucky it wasn't more serious."

I could feel a lecture coming on. So far I'd managed

to avoid any big ones. I think Mom was too thankful to have me back in one piece to get real mad. But Mr. Shonkwiler wasn't that softhearted.

"I hope you've learned your lesson, Joshua. Every year the railroad police give an assembly about train safety. We just didn't have it soon enough for you."

I wished Wendell would get back with the crutches. Mr. Shonkwiler was making me very uncomfortable.

"So long," he said. "Keep it under the speed limit."

Wendell was all out of breath, but he had the crutches. He left me standing at the foot of the stairs balancing the crutches and my homework while he took the wheelchair to the storage room.

Mrs. Borthistle came out of the gym and offered to help. I grabbed the railing and stair by stair maneuvered my twenty-pound leg upwards. Wendell carried the crutches, and Mrs. Borthistle took the books. Reaching the top was like conquering Mt. Everest. No way was I going back down for lunch.

I put a crutch under each arm and gingerly made my way down the hall. This wasn't quite as easy as they'd said at the hospital. I was exhausted, and beads of perspiration were beginning to form on my upper lip.

The first bell still hadn't rung, so Wendell helped me get settled at my desk. Somehow word had gotten around on the playground about my misadventure. When the bell rang, everybody crowded around me and asked questions. Only Ben hung back. I wondered what he was thinking.

Mrs. Bannister wasn't about to waste any of her precious class time. She called the class to order and launched into grading our math assignment. I was glad no one was looking at me anymore. I just needed to catch my breath. This wasn't going to be as much fun as I'd thought. How was I going to get to the bathroom? How was I going to *go* to the bathroom? The questions whirled around in my mind.

Somehow I made it through the day, with Wendell's help. After school we made the return trip downstairs. He got the wheelchair while I sat at the bottom of the stairs.

Out on the sidewalk, he stopped for a minute. "How would you like an ice-cream cone?" he asked.

"Sure," I said. "But I don't have any money."

"I've got some," he said. "I thought maybe we'd need a treat after today." Wendell seemed to be able to think ahead better than I could.

He pushed me along. The fall colors were really pretty, and it was an Indian summer day, the kind that's perfect for playing catch in the alley. But I wouldn't be playing catch until next spring.

When we got to the King Kone, Wendell asked me what I wanted. "You can spend a dollar," he said.

"I'll have a Frost-King with M & M's," I said.

Wendell got the same thing with Oreo cookies. He pushed my wheelchair into the shade, and we dug into our ice cream.

"Remember what we were talking about this morning?" I asked Wendell.

"Yeah."

"I've been thinking about it today. You said that you can tell someone is a Christian by how they act. Do you have to be perfect to be a Christian?"

Wendell laughed. "Of course not. Nobody's perfect."

"My mom thinks you are," I said.

"She's never seen me when I lose my temper," Wendell answered.

"Does being a Christian mean you get whatever you want from God?" I asked.

Wendell knew exactly what I was thinking. "Oh, no," he said. "You can't just put your order in and expect to get it, like a McDonald's drive-through. It isn't quite that easy."

This was getting pretty complicated. With all of the things that had happened lately, I wasn't sure I was thinking straight. Wendell finished his Frost-King and we started for home. We were both very quiet.

I didn't know whether this stuff that Wendell believed made sense or not. At the moment, I only knew one thing for sure—Wendell was the best friend I'd ever had. I didn't even care what he wore! It was funny, I thought. Mom had said that you can't tell a book by its cover. When I first met Wendell, I thought he was a dull, boring book nobody would ever want to read. But to my surprise, he was turning out to be a best-seller.

"Whenever you're ready, Wendell," I said, "let's head for home."